*For my parents, who always let me draw*

I LIKE TO READ is a registered trademark of Holiday House, Inc.

Copyright © 2013 by Steve Henry
All Rights Reserved
HOLIDAY HOUSE is registered in the U.S. Patent and Trademark Office.
Printed and Bound in April 2013 at Tien Wah Press, Johor Bahru, Johor, Malaysia.
The text typeface is Report School.
The artwork was created with watercolor, gouache, ink, and brown craft paper
on Arches Hot Pressed Watercolor Paper.
www.holidayhouse.com
First Edition
1 3 5 7 9 10 8 6 4 2

Library of Congress Cataloging-in-Publication Data
Henry, Steve.
Happy Cat / Steve Henry. — 1st ed.
p. cm. — (I like to read)
ISBN 978-0-8234-2659-1 (hardcover)
[1. Cats—Fiction. 2. Animals—Fiction. 3. Apartment houses—Fiction.] I. Title.
PZ7.H39732Hap 2013
[E]—dc23
2012006579

# Happy Cat

by **Steve Henry**

Holiday House / New York

Cat was cold.

He went in.

Cat met Rat.

Cat went up.

And Cat went up.

Cat met Dog.

Cat met
Rabbit.

Cat went up.

Cat met Bird.

Cat met
Elephant.

Cat went up.

He went to the top.

Cat was happy.

All were happy.

# I Like to Read® Books
## You will like all of them!

*Boy, Bird, and Dog* by David McPhail

*Car Goes Far* by Michael Garland

*Come Back, Ben* by Ann Hassett and John Hassett

*Dinosaurs Don't, Dinosaurs Do* by Steve Björkman

*Fireman Fred* by Lynn Rowe Reed

*Fish Had a Wish* by Michael Garland

*The Fly Flew In* by David Catrow

*Happy Cat* by Steve Henry

*I Have a Garden* by Bob Barner

*I Will Try* by Marilyn Janovitz

*Late Nate in a Race* by Emily Arnold McCully

*The Lion and the Mice*
by Rebecca Emberley and Ed Emberley

*Look!* by Ted Lewin

*Me Too!* by Valeri Gorbachev

*Mice on Ice*
by Rebecca Emberley and Ed Emberley

*Pete Won't Eat* by Emily Arnold McCully

*Pig Has a Plan* by Ethan Long

*Sam and the Big Kids* by Emily Arnold McCully

*See Me Dig* by Paul Meisel

*See Me Run* by Paul Meisel
A THEODOR SEUSS GEISEL AWARD HONOR BOOK

*Sick Day* by David McPhail

*What Am I? Where Am I?* by Ted Lewin

*You Can Do It!* by Betsy Lewin

Visit holidayhouse.com to read more
about I Like to Read® Books.